Escape from the Forbidden Matrix

FOCUS ON THE FAMILY PRESENTS

— ADVENTURES IN —

ODYSSEY®

NEW SERIES

Escape from the Forbidden Matrix

MARSHAL YOUNGER

{Adapted from the teleplay by
John Beebee, Jeffrey Learned, and Robert Vernon}

TYNDALE
KIDS

TYNDALE HOUSE PUBLISHERS, INC.
WHEATON, ILLINOIS

Contents

one

The Exterminated

HUMAN BEINGS were not created to live in the jungle. Their tender skin isn't tough enough to withstand the sun's searing rays and the deadly venom of jungle snakes. Their movements aren't quiet enough to avoid the notice of hungry predators hiding in trees. Their eyesight isn't keen enough to tell the difference between tree bark and a camouflaged reptile that's ready to strike. Their minds aren't strong enough to fight the madness brought on by months of continuous rainfall. The average human being wouldn't last 10 minutes in the jungle.

But the Exterminator is not the average human being.

*   *   *

He didn't bother to wipe the sweat off his brow. He just let it drip down his face in a steady stream of hot salt. After all, this was the 17th day in a row the temperature had broken the 120-degree mark. But heat exhaustion was the least of his concerns. His eyes were trained on the horizon ahead of him as he steered his pterodactyl-shaped hang glider over the trees. He could smell something foreign to this jungle. Something was out there. . . .

Suddenly a flock of deadly lizard-birds flew in a V-shape toward him. He knew the birds would not break formation to let him proceed, so he swung to the right and calmly let them pass. The Exterminator knew a lot about the jungle.

He had been trained for months in the latest survival techniques—everything from the hunting patterns of the Bengal tiger to the signs that a body of water is infested by dangerous piranha. He had gone through rigorous physical training, preparing his body for this ultimate mission. He'd spent days in heat chambers getting used to scorching temperatures. He'd wrestled with animatronic lions and gorillas, and by the end of the training period he was defeating them consistently. He'd taken numerous tests and correctly answered important questions such as, "What is the best way to survive a python attack?"; "True or false: Crocodiles like to eat people alive"; and "How many minutes do you have left to live if you're bitten by the following deadly spider . . . ?"

He was prepared for the jungle. The jungle was not his problem. His problem was that today he was fighting something much more lethal.

His legs hung down from the underbelly of the fake pterodactyl, his stomach bent in half against the metal rigging. Massive fists tightly gripped the front of the rigging. His bulging muscles poked out from under his short-sleeved white jumpsuit. He scanned the jungle below, using a targeting scope over one eye.

Twenty thousand dollars worth of high-tech equipment was squeezed inside his backpack. Equally expensive laser weapons were strapped parallel to each other at each hip pocket. He wore a wireless headset with a microphone attached. With this, he would speak to the people who hired him to do this job—a dangerous job turned down by many other men who were known for their courage.

The Exterminator navigated the hang glider with one hand while he adjusted his wireless headset with the other. "Home Base, this is Eagle One." He spoke into the microphone in front of his mouth. "I have reached the designated coordinates and . . . wait a minute!"

He steadied his targeting scope and gasped. There, in

a clearing in the distance, was a large metallic disk. A flying saucer! He took a deep breath and squinted at the enemy spacecraft. He knew this was the inevitable conclusion to his mission, but he hadn't expected it to come so quickly. He had prepared to survive in the jungle for a month, if necessary, while waiting for the enemy's arrival. But they had beaten him to the punch. This would make the fight all the more difficult. Only the enemy knew the terrain.

"I have a visual," he said into the microphone. "Looks like they've infested this place. I recommend—"

Suddenly he heard an explosion, and his glider was rocked by an energy torpedo. It ripped through the wing as if it were tearing a piece of paper. The jolt broke the Exterminator's grip. He let go of the metal bar, and, for a split second, he hung on to the rigging by his neck.

Flinging his arms up in desperation, he grabbed hold of the bar with one pinkie finger, then pulled the rest of his hand on with it. As he started to regain control of the glider, he heard another explosion.

Two more torpedoes streaked up from the trees. The first flew past him harmlessly, but the second trained on the other wing and struck it with a vengeance. The frame folded in half, then broke off. There was little more left to the glider than the metal rigging. It went into a rapid tailspin.

4 escape from the forbidden matrix

Gritting his teeth, he pulled a rip cord and the rigging fell away from him. But for some reason, he had no parachute. He began a free fall toward the trees below, peering down only for a moment to see the jungle hurtling toward him. All that expensive equipment was no longer any use to him. He had to use his wits. . . .

The trees greeted him with fierce, jagged branches and thick vines that could choke a falling rhinoceros. Impact was approaching.

Thwap! He threw out his hands and grabbed hold of a vine. It broke off at one end and swung him through the branches and away from the ground. In a gigantic sweep, he flew through the air and let go at the peak of the upswing, flying through the air with the grace of an eagle, then executing a perfect-10 swan dive into the small lake below.

The jungle lay still for a moment. The ripples from the dive expanded, then disappeared into the banks. Suddenly, the Exterminator's head poked up above the water's surface. As his body emerged from the water, he immediately sprang into defense mode. His weapon was at the ready—the Sprayboy 4000. It was attached by hoses to two shiny chrome tanks that were strapped to his back. Inside the tanks was a deadly green liquid created specifically for a certain enemy. Weeks before, this enemy had stormed the Exterminator's headquarters and destroyed all the liquid—or so the enemy thought.

All was silent as the Exterminator stood in waist-high water and scanned the shoreline. He pointed his powerful weapon in front of him, expecting an attack at any moment.

A heavy fog was settling over the jungle.

Snap! He whirled around at the sound of the broken twig, only to catch a glimpse of a dark figure slinking behind a dead tree. The Exterminator pointed his weapon toward it but didn't shoot. He knew he was a sitting duck in the waist-high water, so he went on the offensive.

He quickly waded out of the water and ran to the tree, pressing his back against it. It was the only thing separating him and his sworn enemy.

He glanced down and noticed that the roots of the tree had been eroded by the water, which gave him an idea. Slinging the Sprayboy 4000 over one shoulder, he stepped back and threw his weight into the trunk. He pushed hard until the roots tore out of the ground and the massive tree toppled over. It took down the tall grass and smaller trees behind it, too. And there stood the enemy.

From out of the shadows, the hideous creature stepped forward and stretched out to its full length. It was an insect—a wasplike alien creature in a space suit.

Its eyes were like bowling balls; its mouth was like a cave with sharpened stalactites and stalagmites. It had four segmented arms, each segment twisted at an unnatural angle. It stood on its hind legs. Its eyes were level with the Exterminator's eyes. Smoke poured out of its nostrils as it snarled at the sight of him.

"Insectoid!" the Exterminator said under his breath. "I hate Insectoids!"

The two glared at each other. Then the Insectoid used one of its lower arms to calmly and inconspicuously scoop up a fistful of mud. It flung it, splattering mud on the chest of the Exterminator's white jumpsuit.

That was the wrong move. The Exterminator took a lot of pride in his clothes. His jaw tightened in rage as he lifted his Sprayboy 4000 from his side.

"You did that on purpose, you ugly bug!" he yelled. "You knew this was dry clean only, didn't you? You're going down!"

The Exterminator aimed his weapon at the bug and reached for a knob on the tank in his backpack. The outside of the tank read, "Terrestrial Strength Bug Spray."

The Insectoid couldn't read English, but it knew the color and scent of that spray. It wondered how the Exterminator had been able to dredge up more of this lethal poison. The Insectoid thought it had gotten rid of it all!

Fear gripped the Insectoid. It couldn't move. Though frozen in place, it was shaking like a quivering bowl of pudding. As the Insectoid waited to be killed, it cowered with its head bent beneath its two upper arms. The Exterminator had no idea that the Insectoid had a family at home. He didn't know and didn't care.

He took aim. "You're exterminated!"

He pulled the trigger and out poured . . . a pathetic little puff of green smoke. The weapon wheezed like a sick cat, then sputtered and died. The Insectoid peeked out from under one hand.

"Whoops," the Exterminator said in a voice three octaves higher than normal.

He grinned sheepishly at the Insectoid and examined the weapon. He shook it, bashed it on its side, and took aim again.

"OK. . . . Got it now!" His voice deepened to its normal tone as he took aim once again. "Pasta la vista, bug!"

He pulled the trigger.

The weapon coughed, expelled an even smaller puff of green smoke, and died again.

The Insectoid's head straightened up. He relaxed and slowly began to advance.

The Exterminator pulled the weapon back and inspected the barrel. *The mud from the lake must have clogged it,* he thought.

Desperately blowing into the barrel, he glanced up and noticed the Insectoid inching closer and closer. The Exterminator stepped back toward the lake.

He pulled the tank out of his backpack and found the cap. He would just have to pour the bug spray on the Insectoid. But the cap was jammed! He couldn't budge it.

"Just one second. That's all I need," he pleaded, but the Insectoid confidently continued forward. Suddenly vines dropped down in a circle around the Exterminator. He looked up to see five other Insectoids rappelling down the vines, surrounding him.

The Exterminator frantically tugged at the screw-on cap with both hands, but to no avail. Without the bug spray, he had no way of fending off the Insectoids, and now it was too late to run.

"Oh, come on, you guys," the Exterminator pleaded in a boyish whine. His jungle training wasn't doing him much good now.

In sync with one another, the Insectoids reached back and found their own weapons—photon laser rifles. They stopped and took aim.

"This isn't even fair!" yelled the Exterminator. "It's cheating!"

The Insectoids didn't respond, instead silently reaching for their triggers. The Exterminator stared down each barrel in turn.

"That's what it is! Cheating!"

The Insectoids pulled their triggers and a flash of brilliant light illuminated the jungle. A sizzling sound echoed through the trees.

The last thing the Exterminator saw were the words "Game Over" filling the sky above him.

DYLAN TAYLOR threw his joystick on the table next to the computer. "It cheated!" His voice echoed throughout the lab at Whit's End. "That's what it did— cheated!" Twelve-year-old Dylan pulled at his head of brown hair and pounded his fist near the keyboard.

"Dylan," said his friend Sal Martinez, touching him on the shoulder, "the game didn't cheat. Your Sprayboy 4000 got clogged. That's part of the game. You shouldn't have swung into the lake."

"I had no choice," Dylan said, exiting the video game. "If I hadn't, I would've hit the ground and broken my neck. They didn't even give me a parachute. I couldn't win. It's dumb!"

"Don't worry about it. It's just a game."

"Exactly! And the whole idea behind a *game* is that you're supposed to have a chance to *win!*"

"You're getting kind of emotional about this," Sal said, concerned. "Do you really think you oughta play *Insectoids* as much as you do?"

"Are you serious? It's just the best computer game ever."

"Yeah, but there are lots of other things to do. You know, like playing ball, riding bikes, and going on hikes."

Dylan gave Sal a knowing smile. "You're still on level four, aren't you?"

Sal bowed his head and confessed. "Yes! I can't get past the Insectoid patrol." He looked at Dylan. "How do you do it?"

Dylan patted Sal on the back like a wise teacher to his naive student. "Practice, Sal. Lots and lots of practice." Sal pushed up his baseball cap and scratched his olive-skinned forehead. His jet black hair scrunched up under the brim.

Dylan started to load the game again. A catchy tune began to play, and the word *Insectoids* appeared on the screen in neon green letters against a black background.

"Which is why level seven drives me crazy," Dylan

escape from the forbidden matrix

continued. "There's got to be some way out of the Insectoid ambush! But what?"

Suddenly, a voice came from out of nowhere. "Have you tried, perchance, the antigravity boots?"

"Well, no, I—"

Suddenly, Sal and Dylan realized someone was *very* close by. A vision of Insectoids appearing without warning popped into their heads.

"Yaaaaaah!" they shouted, flying up out of their seats.

Eugene Meltsner leaned forward from behind them and, without fanfare, ejected the *Insectoids* CD-ROM from its drive. Eugene was the resident genius in Odyssey. He'd been a college student in town for about a billion years; that didn't bother him as long as he was learning everything about everything. One area of expertise was computers. He liked using his knowledge of computers to help kids learn and have fun.

"Eugene, don't sneak up behind us like that!" said Dylan.

"Sorry, but the pursuit of scientific discovery often leaves little room for proper salutations."

"Scientific discovery?" Sal said, regaining his composure.

Eugene's eyes lit up behind his thick glasses because Sal had asked the magic question. Now he would be able to explain his new program to them. He enjoyed explaining practically anything, but to explain some-

thing that he had actually created was especially satis-
fying.

"It's computer science in this case," Eugene said,
pushing his red hair away from his eyes. "And from
what I can see here, you two are the perfect candidates
for my new experiment."

Eugene blew on the CD and wiped it gently with an
antistatic cloth.

"Wait a minute," Dylan said. "How did you know
about the antigravity boots?"

"Eugene, do you play *Insectoids*?" Sal asked.

"So to speak. You see, as a computer expert, I sympa-
thize with your compulsion to play each new video
game that comes along; so much, in fact, that I have
fashioned the Room of Consequence into a virtual-
reality chamber."

The Room of Consequence was one of John Avery
Whittaker's inventions. "Whit" was the owner of
Whit's End, a unique ice-cream shop where Dylan had
experienced a lot of adventures and learned a lot of les-
sons. The Room of Consequence was often used to show
someone the consequences of making a certain decision. Dylan had used it a few times when he was
tempted to make a bad choice. The Room of Consequence had let him experience, in virtual reality, the results of that choice.

"Virtual reality?" Sal asked.

"Indeed! I've linked the *Insectoids* game matrix to the room's CPU, allowing you to play the game from *inside* the computer."

Dylan swallowed a lump in his throat. "You don't mean that—"

"The result is a life-sized, three-dimensional, ultrarealistic *Insectoids* adventure!"

Dylan and Sal exchanged looks. Their jaws dropped in unison and their hearts began beating rapidly.

"Whoa!"

Eugene was pleased that he'd intrigued them. "Care to give it the proverbial 'whirl'?"

That was a no-brainer.

✳ ✳ ✳

Dylan Taylor's fascination with video games had grown over the past summer. As soon as a new game came out, he had little time for anything else. His classmates came back to school with interesting "How I Spent My Summer Vacation" stories. But Dylan's entire summary began with hitting 500,000 points in *Parking Lot Wars* and ended with capturing the evil gopher woman in *Underground*.

Once that summer, while spending the weekend at a friend's house, he played games on the computer for an unbelievable 12 hours straight. His friend was amazed, and he helped Dylan out by feeding him lunch and dinner and occasionally wiping his forehead with a damp cloth to maintain consciousness. After 12 hours the computer crashed, and Dylan, in a trance, continued to stare at the screen and push buttons for another half hour before he realized there was nothing there. That story was told for weeks in the halls of Odyssey Elementary.

Dylan's obsession with video games also had gotten him into trouble a few times. His parents took away his game privileges on several occasions when he'd neglected homework or sleep. He received his worst punishment—two weeks without a single video game—after he got caught playing a handheld game in the church balcony throughout an entire service. Ironically, that day the pastor preached on Ephesians 5:15-16: "Be very careful, then, how you live—not as unwise but as wise, making the most of every opportunity, because the days are evil." Dylan definitely had a little trouble with "making the most of every opportunity."

Dylan had broken the habit a few times, but when the next new game came along, he was always first in line to try it. The newest game to gain popularity was *Insectoids*. Even Sal loved it!

Sal was not your average 12-year-old boy. While Dylan was constantly getting caught up in the latest trend, Sal had a good head on his shoulders about such things. The two best friends had disagreed on a number

escape from the forbidden matrix

of occasions over the years, and Sal usually ended up being the one who was right.

Sal wasn't nearly as good at *Insectoids* as Dylan was, but that was mainly because he didn't play it as often. He knew better than to play a video game for hours at a time.

*   *   *

Eugene opened the door and led the boys into a dark, cold room. He flipped the light switch to reveal a large, empty room with metallic walls and hard-tiled floors. It looked like one of those interrogation rooms where criminals are persuaded to confess their crimes.

Eugene pulled open a door along the wall. He reached in and began to press buttons. He carried a clipboard and pencil, and he checked off items as he went along. Dylan and Sal wandered to the middle of the room and inspected their surroundings. There was nothing special about the room. It looked just the way it always did.

"The *Insectoids* game matrix was the most unusual I've ever seen," said Eugene. "Portions were so sophisticated that even I couldn't decode them."

Dylan and Sal exchanged looks. Eugene was the smartest person they'd ever known—especially when it came to computers. Even *Eugene* couldn't figure it out?

"Really?" Sal said, looking worried.

"Really," replied Eugene. "And the program was written in such a way that it allows its memory to increase exponentially with each pass."

"Meaning . . . ?" Dylan asked.

"Meaning the game has the capacity to learn as it plays."

Dylan had never heard of a computer learning on its own, but he wasn't worried about it. Sal, however, looked nervous. "If a computer is left on its own, will it be able to tell when something is getting dangerous?"

"What are you talking about, Sal?"

"Maybe we shouldn't do this, Dylan."

"What do you mean? We've got to do this!"

"But if it's not safe . . ."

"I didn't mean to imply that it wasn't safe," Eugene reassured them. "I wouldn't let you in otherwise." Eugene reached into the wall's circuitry panel and pulled out a plastic square. Tiny wires and lights ran through it.

"In fact," he said, pointing to the square, "I've installed this ROM restrictor on the game's protocols to ensure your complete safety."

Eugene replaced the square and checked a box on his clipboard, as if the kids understood him perfectly.

"Nevertheless," he added, "just be aware that there might be some . . . surprises along the way."

This statement thrilled Dylan, but Sal began to look pale.

Eugene punched in a few more numbers and then pushed open the door to go out of the room. As the door was closing behind him, he had one final piece of advice: "Play the game as it's meant to be played, and all should be well."

The door closed with an echo, and the boys were left alone in the room. After a silent pause, they heard the whir of a computer loading, only it was magnified about 20 times. Lights blinked on and off in the control panel.

"You see, Sal? Constricters on the proto-thingies! We're gonna be fine!"

Sal's shoulders relaxed. He looked at the blinking lights and smiled in anticipation. "It does sound pretty fun. . . ."

The beeping and whirring gave way to other sounds: the chirping of exotic birds, the rustle of wind blowing through thick grass, a small waterfall.

Dylan's face lit up. "You ready, Sal?"

"I guess so. But don't forget to show me how to get past level—" He stopped suddenly when something incredible captured his attention over Dylan's shoulder. "Dylan, look!"

The metallic walls had begun to sprout! Vines and trees slithered like snakes coming out of their holes.

Greenery climbed up the walls and across the ceiling. The floor shook, then morphed from tile into a mossy knoll. Green blades of grass curved around Dylan's sneakers.

On the ceiling, through tiny holes in the dense jungle growth, an overcast sky came into view. Enormous birds with high-pitched calls soared through the air. The room seemed to twist in half, and then, right before their eyes, the world turned into a three-dimensional wonderland.

"Whoa," Dylan whispered in awe.

They were suddenly on a cliff, overlooking the fantastic jungle they'd previously seen only on a computer screen. A mosquito buzzed in Sal's ear, and he shooed it away. A crocodile disappeared into the small lake below. Dylan bent down to touch the grass. The blades were coarse and unmistakably real.

The game was about to begin.

three

The Virtual Battle

HUMAN BEINGS were not created to live in the jungle. Not even a fake jungle. But Dylan Taylor wasn't your average human being. He was born to inhabit fake jungles. He taught himself how to defeat virtual enemies. He was the self-proclaimed master of the joystick.

Levels one through six were a cakewalk for Dylan and Sal. Dylan had breezed through these levels when he was outside the computer, and nothing had changed now that he was inside. Sal stumbled through most of it, but Dylan was right there with him to show him the secrets. With power and precision, they mowed down the villains as though they were targets in a shooting gallery. But now came the real test. . . .

Level seven came into view, and Sal and Dylan took off on their pterodactyl hang gliders. With ease and grace, Dylan steered away from the lizard-birds to let them pass. Sal was oversteering his pterodactyl but hanging on. Below them was the virtual jungle, exactly as it always appeared on their screen, only much more real.

They wore shiny white jumpsuits. The front of Dylan's suit read, "Dylan Taylor: Exterminator, player one," while Sal's read, "Sal Martinez: Exterminator, player two." Dylan peered over his shoulder. The tank with the Terrestrial Strength Bug Spray was in his backpack. He knew he would need that.

The fun had just begun.

"Yahoo!" Dylan yelled.

"Yeehaw!" Sal replied, losing his balance for a second, then regaining it.

"Sal, you're doing great!"

"Thanks! And thanks for showing me how to get past level four!"

"Piece of cake! All you needed was—"

Suddenly, an energy torpedo tore through a wing of each glider. Dylan wasn't expecting this so early. The gliders went into a spin, with Dylan scrambling to keep his balance. He glanced over at Sal, who was hanging on with one arm.

"Hold on, Sal!" Dylan yelled.

escape from the forbidden matrix

Several more torpedoes screamed up from the trees and hit with great force. Both gliders fell into a tailspin.

Dylan pulled his rip cord and watched as Sal did the same. The rigging fell away from them as they hovered for a split second in the air, then plummeted toward the trees.

"Whoooooooaa!" they screamed in unison.

Sal panicked as the world flew past him at a dizzying speed. He couldn't orient himself enough to grab a vine to stop his free fall, so he grabbed on to Dylan's shoulders instead.

Even with the extra passenger, Dylan tried to maintain control. As they crashed through the fragile branches at the tops of the trees, Dylan lunged for a hanging vine. Instead, the thick vine caught his foot, which broke his fall but caused Sal to slip off Dylan's shoulders. Dylan hung upside down, his foot entangled by the vine, while Sal held on to one of Dylan's arms for dear life. They clumsily swung back and forth over a small lake. Then the vine snapped, and they tumbled toward the water.

"Aaaahhh!"

Splash!

For a few moments the jungle lay still. Then Dylan's head broke the water's surface, followed closely by Sal's.

All was fine . . . until Dylan felt something slimy on his shoulder. "Snake! Anaconda!"

The slimy thing was wrapping itself around Sal, too. "Ahhhh! Help!"

Dylan flailed wildly as it coiled around his head, covering his eyes. He tried to strangle one end of the creature while Sal strangled the other. They wrestled, getting more and more entangled in its strong grip. Dylan stood up and was about to bite the thing with his teeth when it slipped down from his eyes and he noticed Sal standing still.

"Uh, Dylan," he said. "It's just a thick vine."

Dylan glared at the "snake." He had wrapped his entire body in the leafy vine. He slowly unwrapped himself, smiled, and said with complete conviction, "I knew that. I was just . . . practicing."

Sal grinned, but only for a second.

Snap!

A twig broke in the distance, and Dylan spotted a dark figure ducking behind a tree. Dylan motioned for Sal to follow him, and they waded out of the water. This seemed very familiar. Before they took another step, they both checked their Sprayboy 4000s.

"My weapon's not working," Sal said.

"Neither is mine. It's following the exact story line from before. Only this time things are gonna turn out a lot different."

escape from the forbidden matrix

"How's that?"

"The little cheats are trying to lure us over to that tree where they're waiting to ambush us."

Sal nodded. "But we're not going to be ambushed!"

"No, we're not!" said Dylan. "We're gonna—"

Apparently the exact story line was *not* being followed. Vines dropped all around Sal and Dylan, and six Insectoids rappelled down and surrounded them. *This was not supposed to happen yet,* Dylan thought.

"We're gonna . . . ," he said with a pause, "stand right here and get ambushed." His shoulders drooped and he prepared to be advanced upon.

The Insectoids moved closer and closer, marching in unison and shrinking the circle. Sal and Dylan cowered in the center, standing back-to-back to maximize the space between them and the hideous bugs.

The Insectoids stopped, pulled their photon laser rifles from their backs, and aimed squarely at the two boys.

Sal felt sweat race down his forehead. "Dylan?!"

Dylan was paralyzed . . . but then a flickering thought entered his head. The corner of his mouth turned up.

"Sal . . ." Dylan nudged his friend, who suddenly understood.

The Insectoids lowered their massive eyes to the weapons and felt for the trigger.

Dylan and Sal bent their knees slightly. "Now!"

They sprang straight up into the sky, just as the Insectoids fired their laser rifles simultaneously. Without a target to absorb the blow, each laser shot across the circle and hit the bug on the opposite side.

Zap!

All six Insectoids glowed brightly, then faded away.

Hovering back down to earth, Dylan watched his enemies disappear. Dylan gave his boots a pat of appreciation. "Eugene was right! These antigravity boots are great! Eh, Sal?"

But Sal wasn't next to him. Dylan turned to watch his friend tumble through the branches and land facedown in the mud.

"Well, at least once you get the hang of it."

* * *

Discovering the secret of the antigravity boots proved to be very important as the boys continued on their journey through the next several levels. Once they got that figured out, the rest of the battle seemed to come pretty easily. They were quick to learn that the boots not only enabled them to jump out of the way of oncoming laser fire, but they also allowed the boys to run, jump, and do acrobatic tricks with ease and grace. The Insectoids simply couldn't keep up with them. The

escape from the forbidden matrix

bugs were always one step behind or one second too late.

Dylan and Sal discovered some other handy skills along the way. It seemed to Dylan that it was easier to maneuver and shoot enemy Insectoids when he was in this jungle than when he was punching buttons and moving a joystick around. Here in the jungle, he and Sal were strong, limber, fast, and had dead-on aim with their Sprayboy 4000s. Somehow Dylan had figured out a few complex karate moves in the process too. The weapons were easier to figure out here in the jungle as well. On level eight, the Insectoids were armed with shields that deflected shots from the Sprayboy 4000, but Dylan quickly discovered that he could set the Sprayboy on a higher intensity and destroy the shield along with the Insectoid.

By the time they reached level 10, Dylan had become an expert in every area.

Flying saucers were exploding, and Insectoids were defeated by the dozen. The alien insects glowed, then faded away as Dylan methodically moved from one to the other.

Dylan raced across the jungle floor, dodging laser fire, vaulting off tree stumps, and flipping over the Insectoids' heads with the ease and grace of an Olympic gymnast.

"Sal!" he shouted. "Cover me!"

Sal, who had become quite good at battling bugs, rolled under the onslaught of laser beams and sprang to his feet like a jungle cat, weapon aimed.

Dylan joined him, and back-to-back they sprayed thick, green gas in the direction of the enemy. One by one, the Insectoids gasped for breath, then disappeared.

Some insects got smart and came from different angles—they swung in on vines. But Dylan anticipated that. They were enveloped in the gas, just like the others. They lost their grip on the vines and fell to the ground. Their bodies fizzled and disappeared.

After a few more minutes, the boys stopped shooting. The green gas filled the jungle like a dense fog. They kept their weapons aimed and waited for another round of troops to advance on them.

The gas slowly thinned out, and they could see something in the distance. It was a white flag, flying above the grass. The Insectoids had surrendered.

Sal dropped his weapon and pumped his fist. "Yeah! We did it!" He reached up to give Dylan a high five, but he only slapped at air. Dylan didn't raise his hand. He only gave a half smile, shrugged, and walked slowly to the smoldering flying saucer. His shoulders drooped.

"Wow!" Sal said. "That was great, eh, Dylan?"

Dylan took a seat on the edge of the saucer and laid his weapon down on its side. "Yeah . . . I guess."

"You guess?! What's the matter?"

"I dunno. . . . This is just getting kinda boring. I mean, we've had some great battles, but I thought this was supposed to be a game that learns. It doesn't seem to be learning anything at all. It's just too easy."

"It's challenging enough for me!"

"Well, it isn't for me." Dylan had an idea. "C'mon."

Sal shook his head as Dylan hopped up off the saucer and passed him.

Dylan's history with video games was that he was never quite satisfied with them. He would play a new one continually until he mastered it. Then, after winning virtually every time, he'd soon grow bored with the game. He always wanted more. But the nature of video games is that there are a limited number of playing levels. So Dylan would transfer his interest to some other video game until he mastered it.

This, however, was an experience he didn't want to brush aside in favor of another game. He had been given the opportunity to actually live inside this video game. He wanted to keep playing . . . and he couldn't stand the idea that he was not being allowed to play at the highest level.

He led Sal over to the cliff, which ran straight up from the grass. "Haven't you noticed that wherever we go in this world some things feel very familiar?"

"Whattaya mean?"

"None of this is real," Dylan said. "We're still in the Room of Consequence, right?"

"Yeah, I guess that's right."

"Okay, so check this out." Dylan moved the ivy vines away from the cliff face. Underneath was a circuit board. "If we really are in the Room of Consequence, then right over here should be . . ."

"The main control panel!"

The lights were flashing slowly, as if the control panel was on "pause."

"I noticed this earlier."

"And it's always the same wherever we go?" Sal asked.

"Yep. Now, remember how Eugene talked about that safety proto-thingie?"

Sal squinted. "Yeah."

Dylan removed some more vines to reveal a square plastic piece. It was the ROM restrictor Eugene had implanted to keep the game from getting out of control.

Dylan pointed to it. "I think this is the wet blanket that's keeping the game from getting more challenging." Without a second thought, he unplugged it from the wall.

Sal almost had a heart attack. "Dylan, put it back!"

A computer voice boomed out. "Warning! Safety protocols deactivated!"

"Oh, come on, Sal!"

"Dylan, he put that in there for our safety!"

Sal lunged for the plastic square, but Dylan held it just out of his reach. They wrestled.

"I repeat," the computer voice continued, "safety protocols deactivated! Forbidden matrix now compiling!"

"Forbidden?!" Sal grunted as he struggled to reach Dylan's hand. "I mean it, put it back! Eugene said we should play the game the way it's supposed to be played!"

"And we've done that," Dylan said, knocking Sal's arm away from his. "But I wanna do more!"

Dylan pushed Sal back and threw the ROM restrictor over his head. They both watched as it flew into the lake and disappeared.

"Dylan!"

Dylan hadn't meant to completely lose it, only take it out for a few minutes. "Oops," he said with a sheepish grin.

Deep down, he wasn't sorry. He was ready to go into a world that no one had ever gone into before—even if it wasn't safe.

The Forbidden Matrix

four

"FORBIDDEN MATRIX now compiled," the computer voice boomed.

Sal was slouched over with his back against the cliff wall. "You had to do it, didn't you, Dylan?! You just had to do it!"

Lights flashed on and off furiously in the control panel. The vines and trees swayed back and forth as a stiff wind blew.

The computer voice continued. "Game play begins in five seconds . . . four . . . three . . ."

Dylan whirled around to see what would happen next. It looked as if the place was going to explode. "The forbidden matrix! Now we're gonna do some serious *Insectoid* playing!"

"Two . . . one . . ."

Suddenly, the room went black except for a circle of light coming from the ceiling that shone on them like a spotlight. The computer voice was silent. The blinking and whirring ceased. Sal and Dylan could see nothing but each other. Sal stood up and stared into the darkness. His hands were visibly shaking.

As quickly as the jungle had gone away, it began to build itself back up, like a television picture coming into focus. The trees didn't come out of the walls; they were just instantly there. The world was exactly as it had been before, with one exception: there were no visible Insectoids.

Sal relaxed a bit. Dylan was quietly glad that it appeared they hadn't broken anything.

"See, Sal. No harm done."

A screeching noise got their attention, and they whipped around. The Insectoids' spaceship was parked in the field, making the noise of metal scraping on metal. It no longer had smoke pouring out of it. It appeared to be fully operational. A metallic door opened, and the gangplank lowered. For a moment, Dylan and Sal could see nothing come out, but then they heard the marching.

"I've got a bad feeling about this," Sal said.

Like robots programmed for exact precision, the Insectoid warriors paraded out the door and down the gangplank. Something was different about these Insectoids. They had to duck their heads to keep from hitting the low tree branches.

"Dylan," Sal said, "they're bigger!"

As they came closer, Dylan realized they were *much* bigger—twice the size of the regular Insectoids! And these didn't have puny little abdomens, arms, and legs. It was as though the Insectoids from the first game had gone on a high-protein diet, worked out for a couple of years, and come back with giant muscles.

Dylan could picture the smaller Insectoids being picked on by these powerful pests. One of these brawny bugs could probably lift up a little Insectoid by one antenna!

The ground shook as the bugs continued to march. Sal glanced at Dylan with his mouth wide open. Dylan smiled. "No sweat! We can handle this!"

The Insectoid warriors continued to pile out of the spaceship. There seemed to be no end to the parade.

Sal stated the obvious. "But there's two of us and a whole lot of them!"

He looked over at Dylan, who answered the look with an overdramatic yawn. "So what? We've got antigravity boots!"

The Insectoids advanced like creatures that would

escape from the forbidden matrix

no longer be bested by antigravity boots—like creatures that had learned something. . . .

Dylan casually checked the dirt under his fingernails as Sal watched the Insectoid warriors stop their march and begin their next maneuver.

Two Insectoid warriors leaped high into the air, higher than Sal had ever seen them go.

Dylan wondered how in the world they were going to get down from there. Would they just fall down and splatter on the ground? *Maybe the Insectoids on this level aren't as smart,* Dylan thought. He went back to his fingernails.

But as soon as the two warriors reached the peak of their jump, see-through wings sprouted from their backs! They hovered in place for a few seconds, as if waiting for a command from their leader.

Sal's eyes bulged. "Dylan, they've got wings!"

Dylan replied without looking up. "Big dea—" His eyes bulged as Sal's words hit him. "They've got *wings?!*"

The two warriors bent forward at the waist and, like spiders, shot out silken threads. Immediately a sticky web enveloped Dylan and Sal, wrapping them up like mummies.

Dylan and Sal struggled for just a second. The webbing was as thick as rope and impossible to break. Pretty soon they gave up.

the forbidden matrix

In a muffled voice, Sal said, "Did I mention they can shoot webbing?"

"Oops," Dylan replied, unable to move.

"Great," Sal said. "We're virtual bug bait and all you have to say is *oops?*"

"No . . . ," Dylan said meekly, looking up at the hovering warriors. "Take us to your leader?"

The warriors were not amused.

In the next instant, the entire room faded to black.

THE BOYS woke up in a dark chamber.

"Mmm . . . ," Sal said, groggy and scratching his head. He looked around and saw his friend lying nearby. The webbing had disappeared. "Dylan! Wake up!"

"Huh? Wha—" Dylan woke with a start. He glanced around and found nothing as it had been just seconds before. He heard no jungle sounds. There were no signs of the Insectoids. The floor was hard tile again. He wondered if Eugene had stopped the adventure and they were simply lying on the floor of the Room of Consequence. He only half believed this to be true because there was something strange about this room. He got the feeling he had never been here before. He also got the feeling that he and Sal were not alone.

"Sal! Where are we?"

A voice that was definitely not Sal's answered the question. "You're in my control room."

Dylan sat up and spun around to see who'd made this booming declaration.

"W-w-who said that?"

As if someone was adjusting a dimmer switch, the lights slowly turned on. The large room was still dark, but objects on the wall were now visible. The room had a strange combination of modern technology and primitive decor. The top half of the walls and the ceiling were cavelike in appearance, with vines poking up everywhere. Curved, riblike posts extended up to the ceiling, making it appear as though the boys were in the belly of a whale.

But the bottom half of the room resembled the headquarters of a computer software company. Lights and control panels with buttons covered the lower walls.

In the middle of the chamber, there stood a monstrous high-tech throne. A computer keyboard extended out from one of the arms of the throne. Behind the keyboard loomed the silhouette of a giant.

The shadowed head moved slightly as the giant answered Dylan's question. "I'm the one who spoke."

A light above the giant's head grew brighter and

brought the ominous creature into clearer focus. It was a monstrous figure, though Dylan couldn't yet tell if it was human. It wore a loose-fitting robe and a helmet that almost completely obscured its face. Clear tubes came out of the top of the helmet and disappeared down the creature's back to an unknown source. Bluish light pulsated in rhythm through the tubes and into the top of its head.

Sal winced. "Ew! What is that?" he whispered.

The creature noted Sal's look of horror and, like any polite host, tried to make him feel more comfortable. "Oh, please forgive me while I take this dreadful thing off." The creature typed commands on the keyboard with his hands hidden by the oversized robe.

The boys heard the whir of something being downloaded, and the helmet raised up above the head by itself. Dylan and Sal squirmed as they beheld a horrible sight: the giant had no face! It was just a brain, propped up by a brain stem that disappeared into the robe.

Dylan and Sal grabbed each other's shoulders. "Ewww!" they yelled in unison.

The brain acted as if it was sorry for its behavior and began punching more commands into the keyboard.

"Perhaps you'll find this more to your liking," he said, the words coming from a tiny speaker where his head should have been.

Before Dylan could even figure out what was

happening, a man's face appeared over the brain. The giant now looked like a middle linebacker. Still wearing his robe, he had a thick, short neck; broad shoulders; and a completely bald head.

He looked at each of them and nodded politely. "Mr. Taylor. Mr. Martinez. I am the Master Brain, and you are in my Brain Chamber."

Dylan had about a thousand questions, but the only one that came out was, "How do you know our names?"

"I know all . . . ," he said. "Besides, your names are printed on your uniforms."

"Oh." Sal and Dylan glanced down and saw that this was true.

The Master Brain continued. "Gentlemen, welcome to my world: the forbidden matrix. I am delighted to have you both as my guests and would very much like to make you a most attractive offer."

Dylan knew better than to trust someone who had just grown a face right in front of him, but he was still intrigued by the sound of this. "What kind of offer?" he asked.

"You're here because you're game players. I have the power to give you unlimited access to my Game Room, which contains everything you could ever want to play."

"Wow!" Dylan shouted.

The Master Brain smiled. "You may play all day and all night, if you wish."

Sal wondered if there was a catch. "And what do you want in return?"

"I require only one thing . . . your time."

What a bargain! Dylan thought. "OK!" he said.

Sal tilted his head and gave the Master Brain a look of disbelief. "That's it? No quarters. No tokens. Just our time?"

"Precisely."

"Gotcha. When do we start?" Dylan said.

"Wait a second," Sal interrupted, always the annoying voice of reason. "Wait a second! I don't know about this!"

Dylan was appalled. "Sal, are you crazy? This is a no-brainer." He glanced at the Master Brain. "Uh, no offense."

"None taken."

"Dylan, just hold it," said Sal. "Uh, Mr. Brain?"

"Oh, please, please. Call me Master."

"I don't think so. Listen, when we start this, will we be able to stop?"

"Why would you want to do that?"

"Well," said Sal, "what if we wanted to eat, or go to the bathroom, or . . . What I'm trying to say is, will we be able to do anything *besides* play video games?"

"Excuse me?" the Master Brain said.

"Excuse me?" Dylan repeated, looking at Sal.

"You know, like playing outside?" Sal said.

The Master Brain smiled. "Oh, but my dear friend, you can play outside in a video game without ever having to leave your chair!"

"Yeah, Sal," Dylan said. "What's your point?"

Sal looked up at the Brain and made a sweeping gesture with his arms. "Will we even be able to talk to each other?"

"You'll be playing *vi-de-o* games," the Brain said dramatically. "There will be no need for talk or anything else."

"You see, Dylan? We're not even gonna be able to talk! Now what do you have to say to that?"

With only a beat of hesitation, Dylan replied, "Sounds good! We're in!"

"What?!"

"Excellent!" The Master Brain clapped his hands. "Game Warden! The helmets!"

Two elevator-style doors whooshed open, and a man with a hunchback limped in. He looked a little dazed, but something told Dylan it wasn't because he had just hit his head. It appeared the Warden had had this look for a long time. The Warden seemed confused about what to bring, where to go, and who the helmets were for. He danced a jig of indecision in front of the Master

Brain. The Brain rolled his eyes. He had seen this dance before.

"Just give them the helmets, please."

The Game Warden followed the Master Brain's look and finally understood that he was supposed to give the helmets to Dylan and Sal. The helmets were smaller versions of the Master Brain's helmet, with bundled wires sticking out from the top.

"Place the helmet on your head and you will be escorted into the Game Room."

The Game Warden limped over to the boys. At first he seemed confused about who should get which helmet, but then he shrugged as if it probably didn't matter. He laughed sloppily as he handed each boy a helmet and then stood behind them. He pulled a handheld video game from his pocket and turned it on. It rang with a musical introduction, and he was immediately entranced. He started playing it with flying fingers and a goofy smile.

Dylan looked at his helmet and nodded. "No problemo."

Sal's eyebrows furrowed. "What's with all these wires and the plug?"

"They are of no concern to you," the Master Brain said with a smirk. "Put on your helmet."

Dylan put his helmet on without hesitation. It fit snugly. Sal watched Dylan carefully to make sure he didn't get zapped. As Sal began to put his own helmet on, he noticed that the inside looked like the motherboard of a computer—there were tiny wires running everywhere. Some of them were frayed at the end, awaiting a charge. Perhaps these were the wires that would attach to their brains. This didn't sit well with Sal. He held the helmet away from him.

"I can't. Dylan, this just doesn't seem right."

The Master Brain leaned forward in his chair, a look of anger on his face. "You *dare* disobey the Master?"

"You're not my master!" Sal shouted. "And I'm not wearing this helmet!" He flung the helmet aside and stuck out his chest in open defiance. The helmet sparked as it rolled across the floor. The Game Warden looked up briefly from his Game Boy®, then went back to playing. He had that same goofy grin on his face.

Sal grabbed Dylan by the helmet, yanked him down, and tugged on it. "Dylan, take that thing off!"

Dylan grabbed the chin strap to prevent Sal from pulling the helmet off. "Cut it out, Sal! Don't!"

Sal, who was losing the tug-of-war because Dylan was stronger, pleaded with him. "Come on, you're already a master at this game anyway."

The Master Brain breathed like an angry bull. "There is only one master here! And you will obey!" he yelled, typing commands on the keyboard again.

Sal and Dylan stopped wrestling and watched as the

escape from the forbidden matrix

floor tile under Sal's helmet rose up and flung the helmet toward Sal with great force. It socked him in the stomach, knocking him against the wall. He slid to the floor, gasping for air.

Suddenly Dylan didn't see the Master Brain as someone who was offering a fantasyland of video games. He was someone who'd just hurt his best friend. No one could get away with that.

He pulled off his helmet. "All right, that's it! I'm sorry, Mr. Nasty Master Man, but that was really uncalled-for!"

"It's called tough love, Mr. Taylor, and I suggest you learn from your friend's mistake."

"I'm not learning anything from you. And I'm not playing this game if you're going to resort to cheap shots."

"I'm sorry to inform you, but you're too late. You're already playing this game. It has begun, and you're right in the middle of it."

"Not anymore. It's about to end right now."

Dylan rushed over to help Sal to his feet. He no longer wanted to do business with the Master Brain. "Eugene?! Eugene!" he shouted to the ceiling through cupped hands. "We've had enough! We're ready to come out now!"

The Master Brain looked in the direction Dylan was yelling and, seeing that no one was there, found this strategy amusing. He chuckled. "Whatever are you doing?"

Dylan was persistent. "I'll tell you what we're doing! We're putting an end to this game here and now!"

Sal and Dylan both tried this time. "Eugene! Shut down the program! We're done! Please stop it now!"

The Master Brain continued to smile at this spectacle. "You poor deluded boys. . . . This is the forbidden matrix. Only I have control here."

Dylan refused to believe it. "Eugene!" *Why wasn't he answering?*

Sal shouted toward what he thought was the exit from the Room of Consequence, but his voice only echoed back to him.

"This can't be," Dylan muttered.

"Uh-oh," Sal said.

"Warden!" the Master Brain commanded. The Game Warden didn't hear. He was completely caught up in his Game Boy® video game.

"Warden!" he yelled again. The Warden was oblivious to everything except the tiny world he was protecting in his hands.

The Master Brain leaned forward and projected with every decibel he had stored inside him. "Waaaaarden!!"

The Warden heard him that time. He jumped up and with a goofy smile began running around in tiny circles. When he noticed the Master Brain staring at him, he approached. "Yes, Master?"

With a fake sweetness, the Brain said, "If I could bother you for just one teensy-weensy moment . . ." His sweetness faded and he screamed in the Warden's face, "Throw them both into a detention cell where they can get used to their new lives!"

Dylan swallowed a lump in his throat. *Detention cell?*

In the blink of an eye, the cell doors slammed in front of their faces. Sal pushed on the bars, but they didn't budge. There was no way out.

six

Gregory's Escape Plan

THE DETENTION CELL was nothing more than a dungeon. It was cold, damp, and dark. The walls were covered with a brown layer of hardened filth. There was a sickening combination of smells in the air—musty sweat, rotten meat, and dirty feet that hadn't been washed for six years.

Sal and Dylan looked around in horror at what they had gotten themselves into. "Let us out of here!" Sal yelled.

"This isn't fair!" Dylan cried.

They banged on the bars, but the noise only echoed off the walls and made their ears hurt. It was obvious no one was listening. After a few minutes, they gave up.

escape from the forbidden matrix

Dylan sat down while Sal continued to stare outside the bars.

"I'm sorry, Sal," Dylan said without looking at him.

"It's OK," Sal said sullenly. "We just have to find a way out of here."

"I had no idea something like this was gonna happen."

"I know."

"I mean, it's just a video game," Dylan said, shaking his head. "If this happened on a computer, all we would have to do is hit a button, and we could start over. This isn't supposed to happen."

"But it did. Now we have to get out of it."

Dylan stood up and walked back over to the bars where Sal stood. "It doesn't even make sense. They shouldn't be able to do this. It's just a game!" Dylan pressed his face between two of the bars and shouted, "You can't do this!"

"Oh yes, they can!" a deep voice answered.

"No, they can't. And you've got something in your throat, Sal."

"I didn't say anything," Sal said, his eyes bugged out.

"I did," a voice from behind them declared.

Dylan and Sal whirled around and beheld a scraggly, extremely skinny old man. To Dylan, he looked to be about 120 years old. He was wearing tattered rags that fell loosely over his body. Through a large hole in the material, Dylan could easily make out a couple of well-defined ribs. His white beard reached down to his belly button. One eye looked odd, like it was made of glass. The old man limped toward them.

Dylan and Sal backed up against the bars. "Whoa," Dylan said, "wait a minute, mister. We don't want any trouble."

"Yeah," Sal said, "we just want to get out of here."

The man stopped for a moment and studied them with his eyes. "You mean . . . escape?"

Dylan wasn't sure whether to trust the man, but since he was already in a dungeon, what more could he lose? "Uh, sure . . . I guess."

The man broke out into a wide grin. Dylan quickly counted five teeth, total. It was obviously the first excitement to come along for this man in decades. He gestured with his finger for them to come. "Then follow me!"

The old man led them to the back wall of the cell. It was cast in deep shadows—so dark that Dylan could not see his feet as he walked. He simply followed the sound of shuffling feet in front of him. The man seemed to know where he was going. As Dylan's eyes adjusted, he could faintly see the man bend over toward the wall and begin to pound on it.

Dylan looked around to see if any of the guards were

hearing this, but apparently they didn't come around very often. The man continued to pound on the wall until it budged. A three-foot square of brick loosened and sank into the rest of the wall. The man pushed the brick until it fell back.

Sal and Dylan looked through the hole it created. There was dim light on the other side. The man smoothly ducked his head and began to crawl through. Dylan followed. He noticed that the brick had been carved out with a knife or something. The wall was a foot thick. *It must have taken him 20 years to cut through this*, Dylan thought.

"This is it! I've been working on it for months!" the man said as Dylan set foot on the other side, followed by Sal. *He must have had a really sharp knife,* Dylan thought.

Dylan brushed himself off, then glanced around. His chin dropped to his chest. It was unbelievable. The walls were made of gigantic computer boards, complete with large transistors, processing chips, and ribbons of wires. Cooling fans hummed all around them. Beads of light shot through the wires, which were the size of water hoses.

"Wow," Sal said. "We're in a giant computer!"

"It's like Eugene said," Dylan answered. "We're playing the game from the inside."

Dylan could have stood there and been amazed for

another three hours, but they had an escape plan to carry out, and there was no telling when someone would discover that they'd escaped from the cell.

"Let's move on," the man said, reading Dylan's mind. The man led them through the tunnel.

"So . . . ," Sal said, "you got in trouble with the Master Brain too, Mr. . . . um . . . ?"

"The name's Gregory. Yeah, we all get in trouble sooner or later. I told him he'd never get ahead in life." He chuckled. "Get it? *A head*? He's got no face . . . head?" He stopped chuckling and cleared his throat. "He got pretty uptight."

Gregory hesitated at an intersection of tunnels. There were arrows pointing toward "Drive A," "Drive B," "Video Card" and "Modem." He took the tunnel leading to Drive A.

For a man who looked to be about Noah's age, Gregory moved with surprising quickness. Dylan and Sal had to rush to keep up.

"Did you see the helmet the Brain wears?" Gregory said.

"Yeah," Dylan replied.

"That's his life supply. The only way he lives is by sucking the life out of kids."

"Sucking the life? How?"

"The transfer helmets he gives out plug directly into the Brain's time supply."

Dylan frowned. "You mean his *life* supply?"

"Time. Life. Same thing. Something I learned here. When you waste your time, you waste your life."

Sal glanced at Dylan with raised eyebrows and nodded like a father to his son.

Dylan didn't care for the look. "So I like to play video games. What's wrong with that?"

"What's wrong?" Gregory asked. "How old do you two think I am?"

"I dunno, 80, maybe," Sal said, trying to be kind.

"I'm 12 years old," Gregory declared without batting an eyelash.

"No way!"

"Way! I played the games just like you. Thought they were cool . . . really awesome. I didn't realize that while I was playing, my life was draining away. Then one day it was too late."

"Whoa," Dylan said under his breath.

Gregory stopped at a cooling fan and paused. He watched the blades rotate slowly on their axis. He timed it, and with a precision that only came with practice, he calmly stuck his hand inside and stopped the blades. "Unfortunately, it doesn't end there. Take a look."

Dylan and Sal peered through the opening. They saw a wide-open warehouse, filled with rows and rows of dentist chairs. In each chair sat a child, plopped in front of a computer. Their hands were racing wildly, moving joysticks that were attached to the armrests of the chairs. But no other parts of their bodies were moving. Their heads remained stationary, their eyes fixed on the computer monitors in front of them.

On their heads, each child wore a helmet, exactly like the ones the Brain had tried to get Sal and Dylan to put on. The wires on top of the helmets were transmitting tiny bolts of energy from their heads down long translucent tubes that fed into an unknown destination.

There was something else about these kids that struck Dylan. They looked worn out and old. They had dark circles under their eyes, sagging skin, and sunken cheeks. They were obviously still small enough to be kids, but they were kids who had already gone through advanced stages of aging—like 10-year-old grandfathers!

There were dozens of them, all zombielike in their chairs, moving joysticks without emotion or thought. It was terribly sad.

Gregory let them get a good look, then explained what was going on. "The Brain's got hundreds of rooms just like this one: full of kids feeding him—and they don't even realize it. Pretty soon, they'll look just like me."

Dylan looked closely and noticed one boy in particular. It was a brown-haired boy who looked somewhat

escape from the forbidden matrix

like himself. His eyes were fixed like concrete, without a glance to the left or right, and yet . . . his computer monitor read "Game Over." The boy continued to move the joystick back and forth, pressing buttons madly, not realizing that he was not controlling anything. The game was over.

It reminded Dylan of his 12-hour video-game marathon, the one he was so proud of—the story that would be told for many generations. How he continued to play, even after the computer crashed. He had no awareness of the outside world beyond his fingers and the monitor in front of him. It was just like this boy.

Dylan thought about how much time he had spent on video games. And even though his parents limited his playing time, video games consumed more than just the time he had in front of the computer. He was obsessed with *thinking* about the games. His mother would always get on his case about paying attention in church. Much of the time when she elbowed him, he was thinking about getting home and playing another round of *Earthquake*.

Not only did it seem harder for him to pay attention in church since he'd started playing video games, it also became harder for him to pray. His mind was always wandering off to other things, and he would forget what he had just prayed about minutes before.

Then it dawned on him. His father and Sunday

school teacher always talked about how the devil tries to distract you away from doing the right things for God. Maybe it was the devil who made his mind wander in church and during prayer.

Maybe thinking about video games instead of God was putting him right where the devil wanted him to be.

Dylan was sure the devil was very happy about how little time he spent reading the Bible compared with how much time he wasted doing other things.

But he also knew that the devil was no match for God. When the devil tried to distract Jesus in the wilderness, Jesus' words shooed him away like a fly. God had given Dylan the power to beat the devil and the Master Brain and his own addiction to video games. It was there for him to grab, but he had never taken advantage of it.

Dylan looked at the zombie kids and felt both sympathy and anger. He was angry at the Brain for what he was doing. He was stealing their very lives.

Dylan's ears grew hot as he watched the stone-faced kids play. The brown-haired boy in the warehouse continued to guide his joystick, though the game had long since been completed. Well, maybe the game was over for that kid, but it wasn't over for Dylan. He would make sure of it.

seven

The Real Battle

GREGORY RELEASED the fan blades and led the boys through a metallic hallway until it came to a dead end.

"Well, this is as far as I go. I'd come with you if I could. But it's too late for me . . . I've already wasted my life."

"No, you haven't. Come with us."

"I told you; it's too late."

"It's never too late. You can get your life back. I know it."

"I'm too far gone. My place is here now, where maybe I can help kids like you."

"But you're just gonna waste away in here."

"I'd probably waste away out there, too," Gregory said sadly. "Come on, we don't have much time."

"But if you don't come with us, how will we find our way out of here?"

Gregory bent down and pried open a narrow rectangular vent in the floor. "If there's a way out, it's down through here."

Sal stuck his head through the opening. He was looking down into the Brain Chamber.

"The Brain Chamber?" Dylan said. "This is your great escape?"

Gregory explained, "Look, the only way you're gonna get out of here is to shut down the forbidden matrix."

"Yeah, and how are we supposed to do that?"

"Well, there's no way the Brain is going to let you near his control keyboard. So you'll just have to use this." Gregory reached under his cloak and pulled out a ROM restrictor.

Dylan recognized it. "Look, Sal! It's one of those bomb constrictors."

"ROM restrictor," Gregory corrected. "It fits into one of the circuit boards in there."

"Which one?"

"That's the catch. I have no idea. You're just gonna have to sneak in there and try it out until you find the right one."

He handed the ROM restrictor to Dylan. "Great," Dylan muttered.

"Listen," Gregory said, leaning forward. "Before you leave, I have one request."

"What's that?" Dylan asked.

"If and when you get back to the real world, tell your friends about me. Maybe my life can be a warning to them. And it's a lot easier to rescue someone out there than it is in here."

"We will," Sal assured him.

Gregory stepped back to allow them access to the vent opening. "You've got one life to live, guys. Make the most of it."

"Thanks, Gregory."

*　　*　　*

The Brain Chamber was in a similar state as when they had left it. Lights were still blinking, and electrical impulses were still visible all around. The Master Brain sat in his throne. His eyes were closed and his hands were folded. He was smiling, a look of complete satisfaction on his face. Bluish light was pulsating through the clear tubes, pouring energy into his helmet. He sat there, soaking it in as though he were digesting a big turkey dinner.

Dylan and Sal hesitated after Gregory left them, but they knew what they had to do. The Brain was facing the other direction, so Dylan supposed they could at least slip to the ground undetected. He slithered backward through the hole, then let his feet down gently until he was able to touch the floor.

Sal followed, but with more difficulty. He hit the ground with a slight thud. Dylan covered his lips with his finger to signal Sal to be quiet, but the Brain didn't react to the noise.

Dylan motioned for Sal to follow, and they tiptoed to a wall of control panels. There were dozens of buttons, circuits, and lights. Dylan stared at them in confusion. Something wasn't right.

"This doesn't look at all like the control panel from the Room of Consequence," Dylan whispered.

"Doesn't anything look familiar?" Sal answered.

"Wait a minute," Dylan said, recognizing something. "Of course!"

Dylan pulled out the ROM restrictor and found an open spot for it. The hole looked exactly the right size. He lined up the restrictor and gently fit it into the hole. . . .

Zap!

A shock of electricity penetrated his hand and threw him onto the floor.

"Ow!" Dylan said with as much restraint as he could muster.

"Shhh!" Sal said.

But the noise was enough.

escape from the forbidden matrix

"Who dares enter my chamber?" the Master Brain shouted, taking hold of his helmet.

Dylan was still trying to get over his shock. His hand was trembling wildly.

Sal panicked. "Dylan, hurry up and try it again."

"That hurt. You do it!"

"Dylan!"

The Brain removed his helmet and had full view of them at the circuit board. "So! You've come back to play!"

Dylan got up and studied the control panel. *I must have picked the wrong slot,* he thought. "But where does it go?"

"Anywhere!" Sal said, not taking his eyes off the Brain.

The Brain suddenly looked worried. "What have you got there?"

"Just plug it in! Now!" Sal said.

Dylan's eyes scanned the control panel quickly. "Let's see. . . ."

"Hurry!"

The Brain held out a shaking hand. "No, Dylan!" he said in desperation. "I am your master!"

Dylan found a slot and cocked his arm. "Not anymore!"

Dylan slammed the ROM restrictor into the slot. It fit perfectly. The lights on the panel flickered, and the humming stopped. Dylan and Sal looked at the Brain. He stopped suddenly, his eyes bulging out of his head. He was out of breath. He clutched at his throat and leaned forward. He was running out of power!

"I am your master!" he said, like a toy with its batteries dying. "I am your master! I . . . am . . . yourrr . . . maassteeeerrr. . . ."

His head fell like a rock on the control keyboard in front of him. Dylan and Sal breathed simultaneous sighs of relief. The Brain was dead.

Suddenly his head snapped back up. "Just kidding!" he cackled.

"Ahhh!" Dylan and Sal screamed, clutching each other with both hands.

The Brain typed madly on his keyboard, more determined than ever. "You didn't really think it would be that easy, did you?"

Dylan turned back to the circuit board and began to pick holes at random, jamming the ROM restrictor in whether it fit or not. It wasn't working.

"Now what do we do?" Sal said nervously.

"How am I supposed to know? Keep trying, I guess!"

The Master Brain swung aside his keyboard and rose from his throne. As he stepped toward them, his long robe fell away from his body. Sal and Dylan looked on in horror. The upper part of the torso was that of a normal man. But from the stomach down, he was a spider! Six metal legs stuck out of his body.

"Yikes!" Sal shouted.

Dylan's hand flew across the circuit board, frantically trying to find the right home for the ROM restrictor.

"Sal, get out of here," Dylan cried.

"But what about you?"

"Go! I'll be right behind you!"

The Brain crept forward like a spider toward Dylan, each leg moving independently of the others. Sal took Dylan's advice and ran for the ceiling vent opening. The Brain saw him run past, but he didn't seem to care. He was focused on Dylan.

"I must say," the Brain said with sincere admiration, "I am most impressed. No one has ever achieved this level of expertise."

Dylan wasn't moved by the compliment. His hand was in a frenzy at the circuit board. Every few seconds, he would glance back over his shoulder and see that the Brain had inched closer.

Sal stopped and turned. The Brain was only a few feet away from his friend.

I can't leave Dylan, Sal thought to himself. He was about to run back when he noticed something. The Brain had left his throne unattended. Gregory's words popped into his head: *There's no way he's going to let you near his control keyboard.* That was it! He had to get to the control keyboard!

The Master Brain continued his advance, but he didn't seem too intent on getting the ROM restrictor or hurting Dylan. Instead, he had a proposal. "You have the potential to be the greatest game player ever! That is why I am now prepared to make you an even more attractive offer!"

Dylan gave up with the ROM restrictor and faced the Brain. The long spider legs had surrounded him. There was nowhere to run. "Stay away from me!" Dylan yelled, backing up flat against the circuit board.

Sal crawled up to the empty throne and swung the keyboard in front of him. His eyes flew over all the keys, overwhelmed by the possibilities. He knew that when the Brain typed in commands, it was in a series. Never was any one button pressed to make something happen. The chances of pressing the right keys in the right order were remote. His hands were shaking as he prepared to make his selection.

The Brain wasn't finished with his proposal. "The ultimate video game, all for the small price of your time."

Dylan clenched his teeth, and they chattered. "No! I've seen the other game players! You're stealing their lives!"

Sal knew he had to make a decision fast. His hand wavered about four inches over the keys.

The Master Brain said, "Such a pity. At least be reasonable and hand over that silly device." *He wants the restrictor,* Dylan thought. *It must actually do something.* He held it just beyond the Brain's reach.

Sal started to press the *E. But, no,* he thought, *that could stand for "Explode," and that would get all of us.* He started to press the *H. No, that could stand for "helmet" and put one of those brain-sucking helmets on Dylan.* Sal decided on another direction.

"Eeny, Meeny, Miney . . ."

The Brain pulled his two front pincers as if he was ready to strike. Dylan winced and closed his eyes.

"Mo!" Sal shouted as he pressed a button. A bank of multicolored lights hanging from the ceiling turned on. They flashed in rhythm as loud music poured out of speakers in every corner of the room. A mirror ball appeared in the center of the ceiling, and round spots of light moved in circles on the walls. A strobe light kicked on, and everyone's movements appeared choppy in the fast flicker.

The music was unmistakable. "Disco?" Sal said.

The Master Brain whipped around and saw Sal, the spots of light moving across his clothes. The boy had taken over his throne. "What?!"

Dylan saw the same thing the Brain saw, and he smiled. "Sal! Push some more!"

Sal shrugged. "Why not?"

The Master Brain, in a rage, lifted his torso up high on his skinny legs and started moving toward Sal.

Sal pressed another button.

The Master Brain's face was beet red. "Enough of this—"

Sal hit another key. Suddenly, in a flash of blinding light, the giant, menacing spider-man turned into a giant, silly-looking pink bunny. His face stayed the same, but he had whiskers, buck teeth, and two floppy ears. He held a carrot in his paw.

The Brain finished his sentence, but in a small bunny voice. "—foolishness!"

Sal, sensing good things would come of it, pressed some more keys.

Flash!

The Brain transformed into a giant, chubby baby. He wore a diaper and had a pacifier in his mouth. He spit it out. "Oh, please, would you stop?!"

Sal continued to pound on the keyboard with his index finger. He heard a voice. "Sal!" It wasn't Dylan or the Brain. "Sal!" he heard again. He whirled around and saw Gregory hanging out of the vent.

"Hey, Sal! Escape!"

Sal was having too much fun to be bothered with obvious advice like that, so he went back to the keyboard. "I'm kinda busy right now!"

Flash!

The Brain transformed into a giant winged dragon!

"Now this is more like it," the Brain said with a smile.

"Whoops," Sal muttered.

Dylan shouted, "Sal! Not good! Undo! Undo!"

Frantically, Gregory waved his arms, trying to get Sal's attention. "Sal! Listen to me! Escape!"

"We're *trying* to escape!"

Dylan, seeing an opening, ran under the dragon's wing and toward the throne.

The dragon reared back its head, taking a deep breath and letting out a stream of fire.

Dylan turned quickly to avoid the flames. The dragon chased after him.

Gregory was hanging upside down from the ceiling vent, desperately trying to get Sal's attention. "Sal!"

Sal turned to look. "What?"

Dylan joined Sal at the throne, the dragon closing in quickly.

Gregory yelled, "The *escape* key! Push it!"

Sal looked back at the keyboard. He scanned it, back and forth, frantically. The *escape* key?

The dragon approached, its head bent back to prepare to launch a burst of flame.

"Escape!" Sal yelled, finding the right one.

The dragon leaped into the air, spread its wings, and shot out a wall of flame. Dylan shielded his face while Sal reached up and pushed the escape key.

Just as the flames approached Dylan's face, they stopped like a video on "pause." Suddenly, the dragon, the flames, the lights, and the room began to twist and were sucked into a black hole. Like a digital whirlpool, the world around them spun out of existence.

It was all dark.

eight

A Lesson Learned

DYLAN AND SAL stood there, still shielding their faces, with nothing but darkness around them. A cheerful voice piped in. "Good-bye."

Dylan managed to peek out from under his hands and look around. He and Sal continued to breathe heavily. Neither of them knew whether to trust this sudden, literal cease-fire. They exchanged looks.

The darkness and silence were interrupted by the opening of a door. A stream of light poured in as a silhouetted Eugene walked into the room. "Greetings, lads."

Eugene swung the door all the way open. Dylan had never been more happy to see anyone. Both he and Sal ran to give Eugene a hug.

"How did you like the adventu-ugghh!" Eugene tried to say, but he was met by two very sloppy embraces. He lost his wind for a moment.

"Eugene," Dylan cried, "you've gotta unhook that game right now!"

"It's way too dangerous," Sal explained. "There was this Brain trying to suck the life out of little kids!"

"A fire-breathing dragon!"

"Disco music!"

"Gentlemen, gentlemen! Calm yourselves!"

Sal and Dylan let go of him and backed off. They took deep breaths and tried to explain with more clarity.

"But Eugene," Sal said, "those poor kids in there—"

"—were not real," Eugene interrupted. "They were all part of the game."

Eugene casually walked to the circuit board in the wall and ejected the CD-ROM from its slot. Dylan and Sal couldn't believe their ears. It had been so real!

"Wait a minute," Dylan said. "You mean the Master Brain, the Game Warden—that was . . ."

"All a game programmed by Mr. Whittaker and me to help cure you of your, shall we say, 'obsession' with *Insectoids*." Eugene smiled; he was very proud of the results of his little experiment.

"I can't believe this," Sal said.

"So you did all this just to teach us a lesson?" Dylan said.

escape from the forbidden matrix

"Would you not agree it was a valuable one to learn? *Insectoids* was, in essence, robbing you of your time and your life."

"But you said you sympathized with our wanting to play video games!" Dylan protested.

"I do. And that's why I agreed to help Mr. Whittaker with this experiment. Video games can be a pleasant diversion, but they can also become an addiction that squanders away one of God's most precious gifts—time. When you spend your time doing something that does little to benefit you as a person, you are missing out on so much of what God has to offer."

Dylan knew this to be true. He thought of all the fun he had missed out on during the previous summer. While all his friends were swimming and having fun outside, he had been in his bedroom playing video games.

Eugene continued. "There is so much to learn and experience in the world. It seems a shame to spend all your time in a world that is essentially . . . *pretend!* Wouldn't you say that's true?"

Dylan considered Eugene's words for a moment, then remembered the zombie kids. "Yeah . . . you're right."

"That's why in 1 Corinthians 6:12, the Bible tells us that '"Everything is permissible for me"—but not everything is beneficial. . . . I will not be mastered by anything'!"

Eugene continued to program the machine as he talked. Dylan presumed it was for the next kid to come along—and there were plenty of his friends who needed this program as much as he had.

"Of course," Eugene continued, "that doesn't mean you can't play computer games on occasion. The key is to be master over them, instead of letting them master you."

"So this whole thing was your and Mr. Whittaker's idea?" Sal asked.

"Not exactly. Mr. Whittaker and I wrote the game program, but someone else—"

"Eugene?" a voice from outside the room called.

"Ah, come in. We were just talking about you. This is the young man who came up with the idea for the game."

A boy about Dylan's age walked into the room. Dylan didn't recognize him, but there was something about him that looked familiar.

"Hi," he said. "I'm Gregory."

Sal's and Dylan's mouths dropped open. "Gregory?!"

The boy was many decades younger than the old man from the video game, but Dylan noticed something similar in his eyes and hands. This was the old Gregory before he became a slave to video games.

Dylan and Sal shook his hand and thanked him for coming up with the program. "I learned a lot," Dylan said.

"I'm glad. I hope other kids do too."

"How come I've never seen you around?" Dylan asked.

"Up until a little while ago, I barely even came out of my house. I was always holed up in my room playing video games," Gregory said. "Then one day I was sitting at the lunch table at school and everyone else was talking about being on baseball teams, going to Whit's End, building forts and stuff. . . . I didn't do any of those things. So one day I decided to leave the video games at home and come here to Whit's End. I saw all these cool things here, and . . . I realized I'd missed out on a lot. So I told Mr. Whittaker what I wanted to do, and we did it."

"But . . . how did you do it?" Dylan asked. "How did you just *stop* playing video games? Wasn't it hard to quit?"

"It sure was! But I prayed about it a lot. I asked God to forgive me for wasting my life and to help me not to turn on the video games. I got rid of them so I wouldn't be tempted. Then I asked God to show me other things I could do instead of wasting time—and he did! I started coming to Whit's End, I joined a baseball team, and I started reading books, too."

Dylan admired Gregory because he couldn't imagine giving up video games cold turkey. But after seeing how well Gregory was doing, it made him want to try.

"That's really cool," Dylan said.

"Thanks."

Gregory patted Dylan and Sal on the shoulders. "Come on. Why don't we go hiking or bike riding or something?"

"Great idea," they said in unison.

And they did. The three boys spent the rest of the day together, enjoying God's gifts of sunshine, fresh air and trees, time, and life.

And *Insectoids* was never mentioned once.